For Martina, slime queen of Cadiz and Burlington
—F.G.

To Marie, Chico, Dindin, and Martim.
A special thanks to Heidi, Sarah,
Ricardo, and my agent, Teresa.
—V.V.

Text copyright © 2021 by Frances Gilbert
Jacket art and interior illustrations copyright © 2021 by Vinicius Luz Vogel
All rights reserved. Published in the United States by Random House Children's Books,
a division of Penguin Random House LLC, New York.
Random House and the colophon are registered trademarks of Penguin Random House LLC.
Visit us on the Web! rhcbooks.com
Educators and librarians, for a variety of teaching tools, visit us at RHTeachersLibrarians.com
Library of Congress Cataloging-in-Publication Data
Names: Gilbert, Frances, author. | Vogel, Vin, illustrator.
Title: Too much slime! / by Frances Gilbert ; illustrated by Vin Vogel.
Description: First edition. | New York : Random House, [2021] | Audience: Ages 3–7. |
Summary: When oozing slime threatens to cover the whole town,
residents work together to remove the menace, but is it really gone?
Identifiers: LCCN 2020034629 | ISBN 978-0-593-30357-3 (hardcover) |
ISBN 978-0-593-30358-0 (library binding) | ISBN 978-0-593-30359-7 (ebook)
Subjects: CYAC: City and town life—Fiction. | Humorous stories.
Classification: LCC PZ7.1.G547 To 2021 | DDC [E]—dc23
MANUFACTURED IN CHINA
10 9 8 7 6 5 4 3 2 1   First Edition

TOO MUCH SLIME!

BY FRANCES GILBERT

ILLUSTRATED BY VIN VOGEL

Random House
New York

It wasn't really a *knock* on the door. More of a *squelch*. Or a *thwack*. Or a *blerb*.

We shouldn't have opened it.

But we did.
Which was not the smartest move.

We were going to be
in so much trouble.

It was icky and sticky
and sloppy and messy.
It was stringy and
stretchy and gloppy
and gunky.

It was SLIME!
TOO MUCH SLIME!
Where could we hide it?

In the bathtub? Too ducky.

In the laundry basket?
Too socky.

Under our beds?
Too dustbunny-y.

And then we heard it.

ZLERK!
PHLAP!
SQUERCH!

It was coming
from outside.

Slime was oozing, creeping, skulking, all the way down the street and all the way through town.

Under cars.

Over fences.

Filling mailboxes.

BLORB

Flooding flower beds.

PHLOP

Soon, it reached the school. The soccer coach blew her whistle, but the slime would not be sidelined.

The crossing guard tried to stop it, but the slime had places to go.

The music teacher blared a trumpet, but the slime wouldn't listen.

The PTA held a meeting, but the slime had another agenda.

The slime was taking over. So long, library.
Nice knowing ya, gym. It's been real, science lab.

Something had to be done. This called for action.

The whole town pitched in.
Football players scooped with their helmets.

Flerk.

Cooks used
pots and pans.

Slop

The marching band
filled their tubas.

Aroogahfloop

Dogs raced over with their bowls.

Construction workers dug a hole.

WLerf.

Crunchsplerg

Cats ran with . . . (Who are we kidding? The cats slept through it all.)

And little by little, the slime got littler and littler. Until there was just a tiny blob left, which we plopped—*glerp*—into a lunch box . . .

. . . and brought home.

Which was not the smartest move.

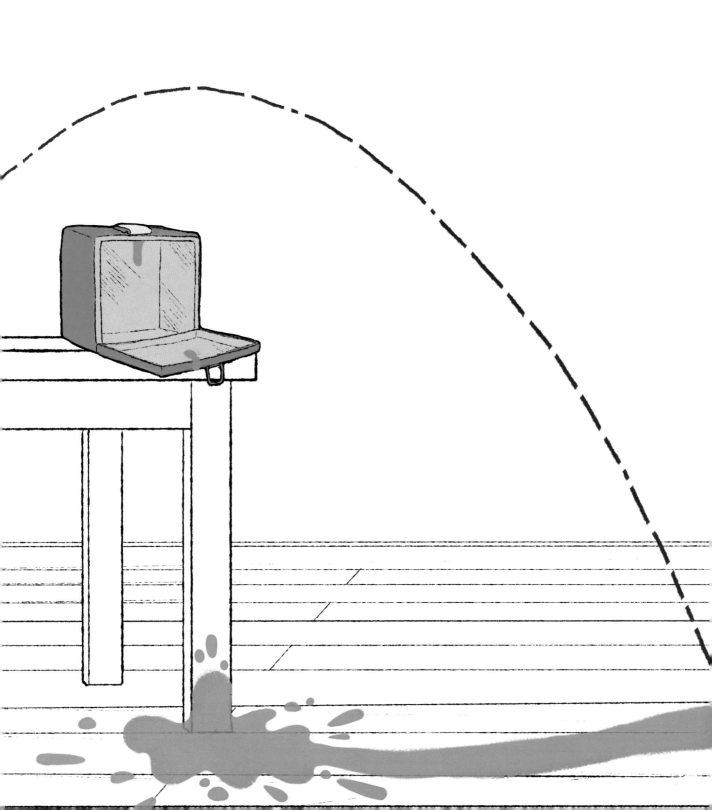

Do you think anyone will notice?